A New Girl

Elizabeth caught sight of a thin, redheaded girl weaving through the tables toward the far side of the room. She remembered the incident in Mrs. Arnette's class and frowned.

Amy saw her, too, and said, "That poor girl. It must be awful to be new and have people make fun of you."

Nora nodded. "Boy, she sure has changed since her first day of school. She was so smiley and friendly then. Now she hardly looks at anybody."

"Well, can you blame her?" Elizabeth said, setting down her notebook. "After that mean trick Lila and Ellen played on her at the mall yesterday, I'm surprised she even came to school!"

Bantam Skylark Books in the SWEET VALLEY TWINS series
Ask your bookseller for the books you have missed.

Sweet Valley Twins Super Editions

SWEET VALLEY TWINS

Out of Place

Written by
Jamie Suzanne

Created by
FRANCINE PASCAL

A BANTAM SKYLARK BOOK®
TORONTO · NEW YORK · LONDON · SYDNEY · AUCKLAND

OUT OF PLACE
A Bantam Skylark Book / September 1988

Skylark Books is a registered trademark of Bantam Books,
a division of Bantam Doubleday Dell Publishing Group, Inc.
Registered in U.S. Patent and Trademark Office and elsewhere.

Sweet Valley High® and Sweet Valley Twins are
trademarks of Francine Pascal.

Conceived by Francine Pascal.

Produced by Daniel Weiss Associates, Inc.,
27 West 20th Street, New York, N.Y. 10011

Cover art by James Mathewuse.

ISBN 0-553-15628-4

Published simultaneously in the United States and Canada

Bantam Books are published by Bantam Books, a division of Bantam
Doubleday Dell Publishing Group, Inc. Its trademark, consisting of the
words "Bantam Books" and the portrayal of a rooster, is Registered in
U.S. Patent and Trademark Office and in other countries. Marca Regis-
trada. Bantam Books, 666 Fifth Avenue, New York, New York 10103.

PRINTED IN THE UNITED STATES OF AMERICA

O   0 9 8 7 6 5 4 3 2 1

To Mia Pascal Johannson

One

◇

"Hurry up, Lizzie, we're going to be late!" Jessica Wakefield called impatiently to her twin sister, Elizabeth. It was a sunny Monday morning in Sweet Valley and Jessica could hardly wait to get to school.

"What's your rush, Jess?" Elizabeth asked, closing the front door behind her and running to catch up. "School doesn't start for twenty minutes. Since when have you ever wanted to get there early?"

"Today's special." Jessica picked up her pace a little. "Janet Howell asked me to meet her at the fountain this morning."

"Oh." Elizabeth nodded. Now she understood her sister's hurry. Janet Howell was one of the most popular eighth graders at Sweet Valley Middle School. She was also the powerful president of the Unicorn Club, an exclusive club of which Jessica was a member. Jessica and Janet had recently had a big argument about the Hawaiian luau party that they were planning. The argument was so big, Jessica had almost been forced to resign from the club. Although the party ultimately went off without a hitch, Jessica was more determined than ever to stay on Janet's good side now. And that meant showing up for their meeting at the fountain on time.

Walking side by side the twins looked like mirror images. Both girls had long, silky, blond hair. Their eyes were the sparkling blue-green of the Pacific Ocean. Everything about them looked the same, right down to the dimple in their left cheek. But that was where the similarities ended. Elizabeth was four minutes older, and even though it wasn't much of a time difference, she often felt like she was four years older. She was certainly more serious, and much more responsible than her impulsive sister.

Elizabeth was conscientious about everything she did. She worked hard in school, loved to read, and devoted a lot of her free time to writing for *The Sweet Valley Sixers*, the official sixth grade newspaper she had helped found.

In contrast, Jessica was entirely caught up in activities involving the Boosters, Sweet Valley Middle School's cheering squad, and the Unicorn Club. Although Elizabeth thought the Unicorns were mostly snobs, Jessica was convinced they were a group of very special girls. She enjoyed the meetings where they sat and gossiped for hours about nothing but boys, soap operas, and clothing. And, since all the members had to wear something purple every day, it was the perfect opportunity to plan their outfits.

"Hey, slow down, you two!" Ellen Riteman, one of Jessica's friends and a fellow Unicorn, came up beside them. "Today's the day Mrs. Waldron's niece is coming to school."

"For a visit?" Elizabeth asked.

"No, I heard she's coming to stay. Can you believe it?" Ellen rolled her eyes. "Just what this town needs."

"Hey, maybe I could interview her for the next issue of *The Sweet Valley Sixers*," Elizabeth said. She was always on the lookout for interesting new stories.

Ellen narrowed her blue eyes. "Why would you want to interview a hillbilly?"

"How do you know she's a hillbilly?" Elizabeth asked.

"Because." Ellen let out an exasperated sigh. "She's from someplace in the Smoky Mountains called Stony Gap." She giggled and added, "Can you imagine a place being called Stony Gap?"

"Yes, I can," Elizabeth replied. "That's where Mrs. Waldron's from and *she's* not a hillbilly."

"Want to bet?" Ellen put her hands on her hips.

Mrs. Waldron was one of Elizabeth's favorite teachers. She didn't like to hear anyone speak unkindly about her. "Ellen, you're just holding it against her because you got a C in science last term."

"Well, it *was* unfair," Ellen complained, as the girls approached the school grounds.

"Maybe if you'd studied a little harder—" Elizabeth began but Jessica interrupted her.

"Oh, come on, Lizzie. Don't lecture."

Obviously Ellen had had enough. At the front steps of the school, she said a hasty goodbye to the twins and ran to join Bruce Patman and a couple of other seventh graders.

"I've got to go, too," Jessica said as she hurried off. "Janet's waiting for me." As Jessica neared the fountain, she spotted Janet in a purple sweater and matching plaid skirt, tapping her foot impatiently.

"Where have you been?" was Janet's only comment when Jessica finally got within earshot.

Elizabeth kept an eye out all morning for the new girl, but by the time social studies class rolled around her attention had shifted to a more important matter—her social studies report. She was anxious to see her grade.

Slipping into her desk near the front of the room, Elizabeth waited eagerly for class to start.

When the bell rang, Mrs. Arnette, who was nicknamed "The Hairnet," stood up and faced the class. "I read your history reports over the weekend," she announced, "and I am greatly disappointed."

She peered meaningfully over her wire-rim glasses and began to return the papers.

"In fact," Mrs. Arnette continued, "I could safely say that some of you never even read the assigned chapters—"

"Yoo-hoo! Excuse me!" a loud voice twanged from just inside the doorway. Mrs. Arnette stopped in mid-sentence and spun around to glare at the intruder.

Standing at the door was a tall, thin girl, with dark brown eyes and thick, red, braids. She was wearing a puff-sleeved green dress with a full, billowing skirt. On her feet were thick green knee socks and worn brown leather shoes.

"I'm sorry to just bust in like this," the girl said, "but I'm looking for my aunt Barbara."

"It's her," Ellen Riteman announced loudly from the back of the room. "The hillbilly!"

Ignoring Ellen's comment, Mrs. Arnette went on. "Now see here, young lady, this is a classroom!"

"Well, heck, I know that!" the girl said. "My aunt Barbara Waldron teaches science here. I'm Ginny Lu Culpepper. Y'see, Aunt Barbara was supposed to meet me at the bus depot," Ginny Lu explained, "but we got in early, so I decided to come straight here."

Ellen Riteman chose just that moment to get up and sharpen her pencil. Keeping her back turned to Ginny Lu and Mrs. Arnette, she crossed her eyes and did a bucktoothed impression of Ginny Lu which made the rest of the class burst into laughter.

Ginny Lu turned around and noticed Ellen at the sharpener. She leaned forward and whispered loudly, "I think they're all laughing at you 'cause your slip's showing."

Ellen looked quickly down at her dress and her face turned a bright pink. A white strip of lace showed just beneath her skirt. Someone in the back row let out a loud guffaw and even Elizabeth found herself stifling a giggle.

Mrs. Arnette clapped her hands together sharply. "Class! Silence!" Then she turned to face Ginny Lu.

"Young lady, don't they teach you manners where you come from?"

"Yes, ma'am," Ginny Lu mumbled.

"I'm sure your aunt would be appalled by your behavior and I certainly won't stand for it! Now march yourself down to the principal's office," Mrs. Arnette commanded, "and straighten this mess out."

Ginny Lu turned to leave. "I'm sorry, ma'am," she whispered just before slipping out into the hall. The door clicked shut and a buzz of chatter went around the room.

"It serves that hillbilly right for trying to embarrass me!" Elizabeth heard Ellen say.

When class ended, Elizabeth hurried down the hall hoping to find Ginny Lu and introduce herself. As she rounded the corner toward the principal's office, she was practically run over by Jessica, who grabbed her arm and pulled her toward an alcove.

"Elizabeth, I have to talk to you." Jessica's face was red and she was out of breath. "I ran all the way from P.E. Boy, am I in trouble!"

"Jess, what's the matter? Tell me what happened."

Jessica looked up and down the hallway and then whispered, "You know Dad's lucky tennis racket?"

"The metal one he keeps in the front closet?"

"Yes, that one. Well . . ." Jessica swallowed hard. "It's gone."

"You mean stolen?" Elizabeth's eyes widened.

"No. I lent it to Janet Howell."

"Jessica, how could you! You know that's Dad's prize possession. He said we were never to use it."

Jessica shrugged. "I know that, but Janet was in trouble. She had a tennis date yesterday with Derek Willoughby, a really cute ninth grader. She forgot her racket and since the tennis courts are so close to our house . . ."

"She asked if she could borrow one and you lent her Dad's favorite racket."

Jessica nodded guiltily.

"Well, ask for it back."

"That could be a problem," Jessica said hesitantly. "Janet's brother ran over it with the lawn mower."

"Oh, no. Jessica, that's awful!"

"I know!"

Elizabeth looked confused. "She should replace it then."

"She did." Jessica had been holding a bag in one hand. She reached into it and pulled out a slightly warped wooden racket. "I told Janet that it was just an old racket that Dad had lying around. I had no idea this was going to happen. Oh, Lizzie, what am I going to do?"

Their father, who was usually warm and funny, had no sense of humor when it came to his tennis racket.

Elizabeth put her arm around her sister. "Jess, I think you're going to have to buy Dad a new racket exactly like the old one before he finds out about this."

Jessica's chin quivered. "That's the bad part. I found out that Dad's racket cost fifty dollars!"

"Fifty dollars!" Elizabeth repeated. "That's awful!"

Jessica nodded miserably.

"Do you have any money at all?" Elizabeth already knew the answer to that question.

"No," Jessica answered. "I bought those new Johnny Buck tapes last week and that lavender sweater the week before."

"Well, the one good thing is, Dad has a business trip this weekend so he won't be playing tennis."

"That gives me two weeks."

"And anything can happen in two weeks!" Elizabeth put her arm around her sister. "Don't be discouraged, Jess. I'll help you figure something out."

"Thanks, Lizzie." Jessica hugged her twin tightly. "You're the best."

Elizabeth watched her sister trudge away and got a sinking feeling in her stomach. *How is she going to get out of this one?* she asked herself.

Two

◇

After school ended for the day, Mrs. Waldron drove Ginny Lu back to her new home. Ginny Lu stared glumly out the window of her aunt's station wagon. The day couldn't have gone worse for her.

She could still hear Mrs. Arnette's angry voice sending her to the principal's office. The shrill laughter of the others as she turned to leave the classroom still rang in her head. She let out a tired sigh and sank back against the seat.

"Penny for your thoughts," her aunt said, glancing over at Ginny Lu.

"Boy, Aunt Barbara, today was one of the worst days of my entire life," Ginny Lu declared. "And that Mrs. Arnette is the meanest teacher I've ever met!"

"That bad, huh?" Mrs. Waldron nodded with sympathy and patted Ginny Lu on the knee. "I know it's not going to be easy getting used to this big school. You just have to give it a chance. Besides, that old house of mine is just too big for one person. It'll be nice to have some company again."

Ginny Lu nodded. Her uncle Pete had died several years ago and she figured her aunt must be pretty lonely.

"It's important to give you some of the advantages your mother and I never had," her aunt continued.

Ginny Lu smiled at her aunt and noticed for the first time how much she looked like her mother. The only difference was the way they wore their hair. Her aunt's was short and stylish while her mother's hung long and straight. But they had the same sparkling blue eyes and warm, open smile.

"And we'll start tomorrow by buying you some new clothes," her aunt announced.

"Oh, Aunt Barbara, that would be great!"

The car turned the corner and pulled into the circular driveway in front of a big white stucco house with a red tile roof. Ginny Lu sat straight up in the seat and stared. "Is this whole place your house?"

Mrs. Waldron nodded, her eyes twinkling. "It sure is. The whole thing. Now, come on in and take a look at your room."

When Ginny Lu stepped into her new bedroom she gasped loudly. "It looks like one of those fancy doll houses in the mail-order catalogs."

The room had been done completely in blue and white. Even the wallpaper was patterned with tiny blue-and-white roses. Ginny Lu ran around the room, inspecting every nook and cranny.

"Is this really my very own room?" She had to blink to hold back her tears.

Mrs. Waldron grinned and nodded. Ginny Lu wrapped her arms around her aunt, hugging her as tightly as she could.

"Aunt Barbara, it's so beautiful!" She shook her head in amazement.

"I'm just glad I could do this for you." Mrs. Waldron smoothed her hand over Ginny Lu's hair. "I hope you won't miss home too much. Your mother and I agreed that you could call her once a week."

The hopeful look on Ginny Lu's face made Mrs. Waldron burst out laughing. "OK, you can call her right now."

Ginny Lu let out a loud whoop. "I'd better call her before I wake up and find out this is all just a dream."

*   *   *

That night Jessica and Elizabeth met in the kitchen for a conference before dinner.

"What have you decided to do?" Elizabeth asked, leaning against the kitchen counter.

Jessica made sure that no one was nearby. Then she whispered, "I'm going to ask Dad for an advance on my allowance."

"You mean you're going to tell him about the tennis racket?"

Jessica's eyes widened. "Are you kidding? Of course not. I'm going to tell him it's for a sweater."

"But will that be enough money to buy a new racket?"

"No." Jessica shook her head. "But it will cover the down payment."

"Hey, you two," Mrs. Wakefield said as she entered the kitchen followed by Steven and Mr. Wakefield. "Time to set the table."

"That's what we were just about to do, Mom." Jessica moved quickly to the silverware drawer. "Is there anything else you need?"

Elizabeth covered the grin on her face with her hand. Jessica was already turning on the charm.

Steven, their fourteen-year-old brother, raised an eyebrow. "Jessica must want something," he announced. "She's being too nice."

*   *   *

Jessica was attentive to her father all during dinner. "Here you go, Daddy," she said as she placed a huge piece of crumbcake and a steaming cup of coffee in front of him at the end of the meal.

Steven rolled his eyes. Jessica never called their father "Daddy" unless she was about to ask him for something.

"Oh, I almost forgot," Jessica said, as she sat back down at the big oaken table. "I found the most incredible sweater today."

She paused just long enough to wait for Mr. Wakefield's reaction. He smiled pleasantly but said nothing.

"And I thought I should get it because I've been needing one."

"You just bought that violet one with the unicorn on it a few weeks ago," Mrs. Wakefield said.

"Yeah," Steven agreed. "Why do you need another one?"

Jessica shot her brother a withering look, then smiled back at her parents innocently. "Oh, that sweater. It's such a confining color."

Mr. Wakefield reached for his coffee cup. "That's why we give you an allowance." He took a long sip. "Just so you can buy these special things for yourself."

"But I already spent my allowance."

"Well, you'll just have to save up some more until you have enough."

"There isn't time for that!" Her parents both looked up and Jessica quickly corrected herself. "I mean, it's on sale and, well . . . it probably won't be there for long."

"I'm sorry, Jessica." Her father shook his head. "The reason we give you kids an allowance is so you can learn how to budget yourselves."

Mrs. Wakefield nodded. "You should follow your sister's example. How long have you been saving for those riding boots, Elizabeth?"

Elizabeth deliberately avoided her twin's eyes and murmured, "Three months."

A big tear had begun to roll down Jessica's cheek but the news of Elizabeth's savings made her eyes brighten. Hastily she wiped the tear away.

Elizabeth saw the change in her sister and knew exactly what was coming next. There was no way she was going to give in this time.

Jessica waited until the dishes were rinsed and loaded. Then she turned to her sister. "Lizzie, would you do me a teensy favor?"

Elizabeth gathered her courage. It was never easy to say no to Jessica. She could be very persuasive.

Elizabeth looked her sister squarely in the eye. "Forget it, Jess. I've waited too long for these boots. I'm not giving you my savings."

"I'm not asking you to give it to me. I just need a little loan."

"A loan means you pay me back, you know," Elizabeth retorted.

"I know that. Pretty please? You *have* to help me. I'll be in such big trouble if Dad finds out."

Elizabeth felt herself start to weaken. "When did you say you were ordering the racket?"

"Tomorrow."

"Well . . . Maybe I can lend you enough for the down payment," Elizabeth said. "But that's all."

"I knew you'd help me. You're wonderful!" Jessica threw her arms around her sister.

"But remember, you still have to pay me back *and* earn the rest of the money to pick up the racket."

"That's two weeks away." Jessica dismissed the problem with a wave of her hand. "I'll think of something by then." She turned and dashed for the door.

Elizabeth leaned against the counter and sighed. She had a sinking feeling she would never see that money again. And, she thought with a smile, wasn't it just like Jessica to run off and leave her to finish cleaning up.

Three

◇

"Wow, Aunt Barbara, I've never seen so many mirrors in one place!"

Ginny Lu Culpepper stood in the middle of the gallery at the Sweet Valley Mall on Tuesday afternoon. The escalators leading to the second floor were circled by tall pillars covered with mirrors. Light bounced off the glass in a dazzling display.

"It looks like a magical kingdom!"

Mrs. Waldron laughed and gently guided her niece through the crowd of shoppers. They stopped in front of a small dress shop with silver mannequins in the window.

"This is Valley Fashions," her aunt announced.

"It seems to be pretty popular with the girls at school."

"That's right," a voice said from behind them. "It's the only place to shop."

Ginny Lu spun around and saw a vaguely familiar dark-haired girl standing by the window.

"Are you shopping for yourself, Mrs. Waldron?" the girl asked politely.

"Goodness, no!" Ginny Lu's aunt replied with a chuckle. "I decided to help my niece pick out a few new things for school. Ellen Riteman, I'd like you to meet Ginny Lu Culpepper."

"We've met," Ellen said curtly.

"Oh?" Mrs. Waldron said.

"Yesterday," Ellen explained, her eyes fixed steadily on Ginny Lu. "In Mrs. Arnette's class."

"Oh, that's right." Ginny Lu snapped her fingers. "You're the one whose slip was showing."

Ellen frowned. "Yes. Thanks for pointing that out to me."

"Aw, it was nothing." Ginny Lu looked down at her feet and then back at Ellen with a big grin. "Just trying to help."

"Mrs. Waldron, I've got an idea," Ellen said suddenly. "Why don't I help Ginny Lu shop? I'm sure I can find her an outfit that's just right for her."

"Well, that's awfully nice of you, Ellen. I'm

pretty old-fashioned when it comes to what you girls are wearing these days." Mrs. Waldron looked at Ginny Lu. "I have some errands I can run while you two girls shop."

"Just leave it to me," Ellen said, "and when you come back, Ginny Lu can model for you."

"How's that sound to you, Ginny Lu?" her aunt asked.

Ginny Lu could only nod excitedly. Maybe things were going to work out after all. Ellen was going to help her find the perfect outfit for Sweet Valley. Now she'd be sure to fit in!

"OK, honey." Her aunt gave her arm a squeeze. "See you in twenty minutes!"

"Come on, then!" Ellen pushed open the glass door to Valley Fashions and led Ginny Lu inside.

"They sure don't have stores like this in Stony Gap," Ginny Lu said, as Ellen led her toward the back of the store.

"I'm sure they don't," Ellen echoed heartily. She stopped at a rack marked CLOSEOUTS and began flipping through it. "Now, the secret to dressing well is finding clothes that reflect your personality."

"Oh, boy," Ginny Lu mumbled. "I wouldn't know where to begin."

"That's why I'm going to help you." Ellen looked her straight in the eye. "Just like you helped me yesterday." She thrust some hangers into Ginny Lu's arms. "Here, try these on."

"Gee, some of these are a little wild." Ginny Lu pointed to a pair of tights with a leopard-skin pattern. "I don't think they're me at all!"

"Don't be silly," Ellen said confidently. "You're in California now. We do things differently here."

A tinny laugh rippled across from the front of the shop. "Ellen Riteman, what are you *doing* with those clothes? Going to a costume party?"

Ginny Lu looked up and saw a pretty girl with long brown hair looking at them, trying to hold back her laughter.

"Lila, what a surprise!" Ellen exclaimed. "What perfect timing!"

"A costume party?" Ginny Lu stammered. "I—I don't understand."

"Oh, Lila is always joking around. Aren't you?"

Before Lila could reply, Ellen said, "Lila, I'm helping Mrs. Waldron's niece find the perfect outfit to wear to school tomorrow."

"Oh." Lila's eyes grew wide and she giggled. "Let me help!" She dropped the bags she was carrying and immediately began pulling clothes off the rack and handing them to Ginny Lu.

Ginny Lu couldn't believe her good luck. She stood in the middle of the boutique while both girls ran around the store collecting outfits for her to try on.

"OK, Ginny Lu," Ellen finally announced, ushering her toward the corner dressing room. "I think we've got everything."

Ellen pushed back the curtain, shoved Ginny Lu into the tiny room, and hung up two skirts, socks, tights, a couple of sweaters, two blouses and some accessories.

"Now, be sure and put these on," Lila ordered as she handed Ginny Lu a pair of earrings that had bunches of bright yellow plastic bananas dangling from a silver chain.

"Hurry and get dressed before your aunt comes back!" Ellen said, drawing the curtain shut.

"I can't wait to see what I look like!" Ginny Lu cried excitedly.

From the other side of the curtain Lila and Ellen chorused, "Neither can we!"

Ginny Lu put on the first outfit the girls had assembled for her. Then she took a look at herself in the full-length mirror. The leopard-skin tights had blue-and-white striped knee socks pulled up over them and the orange leather miniskirt made her knees look even knobbier than usual.

"Gosh, people in Sweet Valley sure have a crazy idea of what looks good!" she remarked to her reflection. The huge green sweater they had told her to put on was at least three sizes too big but Ellen had said that everyone wore them that way. She knotted the long pink scarf around her neck and put on the earrings.

"Ginny Lu? How's it going?" It was her aunt calling from outside the dressing room. "Where's Ellen? I thought she was going to help you."

"She should be out there somewhere," Ginny Lu replied, slipping into a pair of snakeskin-pattern tennis shoes. "Another girl named Lila was helping me, too. Isn't she there?"

"Lila Fowler?" Mrs. Waldron remarked. "My, my."

Ginny Lu could tell her aunt was impressed. She knew she had been worried about her fitting in. Ginny Lu took one last look at her reflection and threw open the dressing room door.

"Well, how do I look?"

Mrs. Waldron gasped and covered her mouth with her hand.

"Oh, no!" The saleslady standing beside her looked appalled. "How dreadful!"

Ginny Lu felt confused. "What do you mean? Don't I look OK?"

"That sweater is ten times your size," her aunt began.

"I know, but—"

"And those colors clash horribly," the saleslady said. "Is your niece colorblind?"

"No, she is not," her aunt retorted. "It's just . . . well, she's from—she's new to town."

Ginny Lu could tell she had embarrassed her aunt. "I don't get it," she muttered. "They told me this is what everyone's wearing."

Her aunt looked very unhappy. "Ginny Lu, have you ever seen anyone dressed like this?"

"No, but—"

"I'm afraid those two have played a joke on you," Mrs. Waldron said gently.

"No, they wouldn't!" Ginny Lu protested. "They're my new friends!"

Suddenly a burst of laughter exploded behind her. Reflected in the mirror Ginny Lu could see Ellen, Lila, and a few other girls pointing at her through the shop window. Their mocking laughter echoed through the shop. Ginny Lu stared at her reflection in the three-way mirror. Her feet felt like lead as she stood there, staring at herself. She squeezed her eyes shut and wished that she could disappear.

Mrs. Waldron turned sharply and strode to the front of the shop. Lila and Ellen were still howling and patting each other on the back when Mrs. Waldron's voice silenced them.

"How could you girls be so cruel? What gives you the right to laugh at someone, just because they're different from you? You should all be ashamed of yourselves!"

No one said a word. Ellen and Lila stood still and stared at the ground.

When Ginny Lu stepped back out of the changing room with her old clothes on, she noticed that her aunt and the girls were all still there. She was tempted to run right back into the dressing room, but instead, she tilted her chin up proudly and marched out of the store. Her aunt joined her and, side by side, they walked down the long corridor to the exit of the mall.

Once they had gotten into the car, Mrs. Waldron turned to Ginny Lu, her eyes glistening with tears. "It never occurred to me that the children would take it out on you because I'm a teacher."

"It's not you, Aunt Barbara. It's me. I just don't fit in. I'm different than they are."

Mrs. Waldron gazed at her niece for a moment, then started the car. They drove the whole way home in silence.

Four

◇

"May I have your attention, please?" The voice of Mr. Clark, the principal, boomed over the P.A. system on Wednesday morning. "Excuse me, teachers, for interrupting your classes, but I have a brief announcement to make."

All the students in Mrs. Arnette's class sat up to listen.

"Mrs. Cunningham, the art teacher from Rourke Middle School, is visiting us today. As you know, the Tenth Annual Arts and Crafts Fair is to be held a week from this Saturday. Mrs. Cunningham helped to organize the fair last year and is here to answer any questions you might have about entering. The proceeds from the fair, as you know, will go toward building improvements in honor of the twenty-fifth anniversary of our school. Students, please stop by the lunchroom to ask her questions about the fair. Thank you."

Ginny Lu listened to the sound click off on the speaker and said out loud, "I'd like to enter that fair. What do you have to do to get in?"

Mrs. Arnette peered over her glasses and said, "You have to have a skill or talent."

"Well, I guess that leaves you out," a voice whispered from the back.

Ginny Lu spun around and glared at Ellen Riteman.

Mrs. Arnette didn't hear Ellen and continued. "Every year the middle schools around Sweet Valley take turns sponsoring the fair and students from all participating schools operate booths and display their artwork. Will anyone here be entering?" Mrs. Arnette asked the class.

"Ginny Lu could enter and model hillbilly fashions," Ellen whispered loudly.

Charlie Cashman, who sat directly behind Ginny Lu, chimed in. "Yeah, she could show off the latest in overalls and corncob pipes."

Ginny Lu was not only hurt, but angry. She bit her lip and listened to the kids around her snicker.

Then she heard Ellen say, "You should have seen our little backwoods girl at the mall yesterday!"

That did it. Ginny Lu spun around in her seat and said loudly, "Ellen Riteman, you be quiet!"

"What did you say?" Mrs. Arnette's smile disappeared as she focused her steely gray eyes on Ginny Lu.

Ginny Lu slumped in her seat. Before she could answer, Mrs. Arnette said, "Young lady, at this school we do not shout. If you have something to say, you raise your hand. Is that understood?"

Ginny Lu nodded and stared as hard as she could at the eraser on the end of her pencil. All of a sudden the classroom was so quiet she could hear the clock at the front of the room ticking loudly. How come she was always the one Mrs. Arnette caught talking?

"Now," Mrs. Arnette said, "let's turn back to page one hundred twenty-three of our social studies books. Winston, will you read for us?"

As Winston Egbert started to read, Ginny Lu squeezed her eyes shut and prayed for the hour to end quickly.

That afternoon in the cafeteria, Elizabeth paid the cashier for her lunch and then made a face at the meal on her plate. "Zucchini casserole—ugh," she muttered.

She moved away from the counter and scanned the lunchroom. Finally, she spotted her best friend, Amy Sutton, having an animated discussion with Nora Mercandy. She wound her way across the room to join them.

"Hi, Elizabeth," Amy said. "I'm glad you're here. Nora just got this great idea for the next issue of *The Sweet Valley Sixers*. It's about the Arts and Crafts Fair." She nudged Nora. "You tell her."

Nora tucked a strand of long dark hair behind one ear and grinned. "I thought it would be really cool if we had pictures of all of the contestants posing with their entries on the front page. Then inside—"

"We would have a ballot," Amy interrupted excitedly. "So the kids could vote for their choices. You know, 'Most Original,' et cetera."

"We could call it 'The Student's Choice.' What do you think?"

Amy and Nora folded their hands on the table and looked expectantly at Elizabeth. Elizabeth munched on a slice of carrot from her salad, mulling the idea over.

"Well?" Amy prodded her.

"It *would* be kind of interesting to see what the students like best, as opposed to the judges. I think it's a terrific idea!"

Elizabeth reached in her bag and pulled out her notepad. "But we need to get started on it right away. First, we need to talk to Mr. Bowman and have him OK it. Then we have to figure out a way to reproduce the photographs since we usually don't have pictures in the newspaper. Maybe Mr. Bowman will have some ideas."

Mr. Bowman was an English teacher as well as the faculty supervisor for the sixth grade paper. He usually was enthusiastic about his staff's suggestions for articles or special issues.

"I'll go talk to him now," Nora said, pushing her tray aside. "I can't find anything edible on this plate so I might as well use the lunch period for something worthwhile."

Elizabeth turned to Amy. "Mr. Clark announced that Mrs. Cunningham is meeting with people during lunch. Why don't you go tell her about our idea?"

Amy nodded and held up her own notebook. "I was just going to suggest that."

Just then Elizabeth caught sight of a thin, red-headed girl weaving through the tables toward the far side of the room. She remembered the incident in Mrs. Arnette's class and frowned.

Amy saw her, too, and said, "That poor girl. It must be awful to be new and have people make fun of you."

Nora nodded. "You're not kidding. Remember what happened to me when I was new?" Then she looked over her shoulder and said, "She sure has changed since she first arrived here. She was so smiley and friendly then. Now she hardly looks at anybody."

"Well, can you blame her?" Elizabeth said, setting her notepad down. "After that mean trick Ellen and Lila played on her at the mall yesterday, I'm surprised she even came to school."

"Those two can be pretty cruel," Nora said sadly.

Elizabeth remembered how mean Lila and Janet Howell had been to Nora when she was new at school. They had spread the rumor that she was a witch just because she lived in an old house.

"I'm going to go ask Ginny Lu to join us," Elizabeth said, pushing her chair back from the table. "I'm sure she could use a few friends."

"Amy and I have to get going on our assignments," Nora said.

"Oh, that's right. Well, I'll see you guys later then."

Elizabeth waved goodbye to her friends and then looked around for Ginny Lu. Just as she stood up to go get her, Jessica appeared.

"You can't leave now, Elizabeth. I just got here."

"I'll be right back," Elizabeth said. "I'm going to see if Ginny Lu wants to join—"

"Aren't you going to eat your casserole?" Jessica interrupted, sliding into the chair next to her. "It smells delicious."

Elizabeth looked at her sister in astonishment. "Jessica, you can't stand zucchini!"

"Well, I'm starved," Jessica replied. "So anything looks good to me."

"Why don't you buy yourself lunch?"

Jessica folded her arms across her chest and sighed. "I can't. I have to save my money for the racket."

"Oh, Jessica," Elizabeth said, sitting back down and picking up her fork. "You're not going to make me feel bad about eating my lunch, are you? If you're so hungry, spend the lunch money Mom gave you and earn the racket money some other way."

"I'm not trying to make you feel bad," Jessica said simply.

"Well, good," Elizabeth said bluntly. "The whole

problem is your own fault and you're just going to have to work it out by yourself."

Jessica nodded sadly. "You're right."

"OK, then," Elizabeth said. "So if you want to starve yourself to save money, go ahead."

There was a long pause. Finally Elizabeth took a bite of her salad.

"I just thought you'd like to know," Jessica said, "that in order for me to buy Dad his new racket, I'll have to save my lunch money for the rest of the year." Her lower lip trembled dangerously. "I may never eat lunch again."

At the sight of a single tear streaming down Jessica's cheek, Elizabeth dropped the fork on the table and threw her hands in the air. She always gave in when her sister started to cry. "You win, Jessica. You can have a bite!" Then she added, "but just one!"

"Thanks, Lizzie," Jessica said, her eyes glowing. She slid her sister's tray in front of her. "You're the greatest!"

Elizabeth sighed and rested her chin on her hand. Within seconds Jessica had devoured her entire lunch—casserole and all.

Ginny Lu picked at her lunch with her fork but she wasn't very hungry. She had tried to eat but every time she looked up, she'd catch someone staring at her. They'd turn away quickly and then she would hear whispers and giggles.

"I can't take this anymore," she muttered under her breath. She stood up and shoved the tray through the return window. Then she walked briskly toward the exit trying not to look at anyone.

Just as she opened the door, a paper airplane swooped by her head and hit the wall with a flat thunk. Ginny Lu spun around to see who had thrown it and was hit square in the face with another one. She shrieked and ran into the hall. The doors swung closed behind her and a ripple of laughter echoed in her ears.

Ginny Lu decided that it would be safest to hide out in the girls' room. *Why do they hate me?* she asked her reflection in the bathroom mirror. She made a face at herself. *Because you're ugly, you don't dress right, and your hair is awful.* She angrily tugged at her braid, then turned away from the mirror and went into one of the stalls.

Suddenly the door burst open and Ginny Lu heard several girls come bustling in. They stood in front of the mirrors over the sinks, chattering away as they combed their hair. Ginny Lu recognized a voice that made her heart stop.

"Oh, Janet, I wish you'd been there! She looked so funny in the store!"

It was Ellen Riteman. Then Lila Fowler chimed in.

"She stood there like a skinny clown and asked, 'Doesn't this-here outfit look goo-ud?'"

Then Janet added, "It's too bad Ginny Lu wasn't here for our luau party. We could have told her to come dressed as a palm tree and she probably would have."

Ginny Lu winced as the girls imitated her accent. She heard Ellen and another girl burst into gales of laughter.

"Didn't she know she was being set up?" the other voice asked.

"No, of course not," Ellen replied. "She's just a hillbilly!"

A wave of humiliation rolled over Ginny Lu, followed by hurt, and then boiling anger. She wanted to leap out and scream at them all but she bit her lip. She knew she would only make things worse for herself.

The bell rang. Ginny Lu listened from inside the stall as the girls walked out the door and clattered down the hall, their voices echoing behind them.

Ginny Lu didn't move. She stood quietly until a perfect stillness returned to the corridors of the school. She tiptoed out into the hall. At the end of the corridor the double glass doors glistened in the afternoon sun.

I've got to get out of here! she thought to herself. Taking a deep breath, she tore down the hall and burst through the exit doors.

Then she ran harder than she had ever run before. She didn't know where she was going. All she wanted to do was get as far away from Sweet Valley Middle School as possible.

Five

◇

Ginny Lu pounded down the sidewalk past rows and rows of trim suburban houses. She hardly noticed that the neighborhood was changing around her.

The modest homes grew into mansions with neatly manicured lawns that seemed to stretch on forever. Then the sidewalk beneath her feet turned into the shoulder of the road and the houses grew fewer and farther apart.

She ran up over a short rise and a warm gust of wind carried a familiar scent that stopped her in her tracks. It was a wonderful smell, rich and earthy, like

Tennessee, the Smoky Mountains, and her family's farm.

Ginny Lu followed the aroma to a lush group of palm trees. A white fence lined a meadow full of green grass. Next to the fence a large wooden sign hung on twin posts. It read "Carson Stables."

"Horses!"

For the first time that day Ginny Lu smiled. She ran to the fence and hopped up on the first plank, drinking in the view with delight. In the middle of it all were several wooden buildings, painted red.

Ginny Lu let out a hoot that echoed off the buildings. She hopped off the fence and skipped up the winding lane all the way to the stable. She leaned back against the building, closed her eyes and took a deep breath. The air was thick with the smell of hay, saddles, and horses.

She walked dreamy-eyed down the long line of stalls, pausing at each one to whisper greetings to the horses. When she reached the last stall, Ginny Lu peeked inside.

There, standing half in shadow, was the prettiest white mare she had ever seen. Its big brown eyes blinked soulfully and as the little mare stepped out of the shadows, Ginny Lu realized with delight that the horse was pregnant.

"Come here, girl," she whispered, clucking

gently to the beautiful white Arabian. "Aren't you just the prettiest little mama-to-be."

The mare's ears pricked up at the sound of Ginny Lu's voice. She stepped over to the stable door and gently nuzzled the girl's cheek. Her muzzle was as soft as velvet. Ginny Lu scratched her behind one soft ear and ran her hand over the mare's sleek mane. Engraved on a little brass plate along her halter was the name Snow White.

"It's perfect," Ginny Lu said with a sigh. She reached both arms up and hugged Snow White around the neck. "I wish I could stay here with you for ever and ever."

Elizabeth decided to ride her bike to Carson Stables after school. That way she'd have enough time to visit the horses and chat with Ted, the stable boy, before her lesson.

She raced into the kitchen and stuffed a paper bag full of carrots from the refrigerator. Then she tucked a few sugar cubes into her pocket and checked her backpack for her riding equipment.

"Riding hat, gloves, sturdy shoes—all there." As she zipped up the pack, Elizabeth thought wistfully of the riding boots that would soon be hers. She looped her arms through the pack, pushed open the front door and got her bicycle out of the garage.

It was a brilliant sunny afternoon. Elizabeth checked her watch, climbed on her bike, and took off. When she reached Carson Stables, she leaned her bike against the porch of the front office, paused long enough to catch her breath, then skipped over to the tack room.

"Ted?"

There was no reply as she stepped onto the broad wooden planks of the big room. The walls were lined with saddles, halters, and bridles of all types and sizes.

"Ted? You around?" she called again.

When she still got no answer, Elizabeth trotted across the dusty road between the tack room and the stables. She paused and listened to the stirrings and rustlings of the horses in their stalls.

"There you go, Calypso," she cooed to the dappled gray as she held up a piece of carrot. She moved down the line of stalls and each horse came forward to greet her like an old friend.

Suddenly Elizabeth cocked her head. Someone was singing in a sweet, clear voice. And it was coming from Snow White's stall. Elizabeth tiptoed to the stable door and listened to the song.

Go to sleep, my little baby.
When you wake, you will see

All the pretty little horses.
Dapples and grays, pintos and bays,
All the pretty little horses.

As quietly as she could, Elizabeth peered around the door. Unfortunately, the white mare saw her and skittered backwards in the stall.

"Who's there?" Ginny Lu cried, leaping to her feet.

Elizabeth stepped forward. "It's me, Elizabeth Wakefield. I'm in one of your classes at school. Mrs. Arnette's."

"Oh." Ginny Lu peered out timidly from the shadows. "I recognize you. You're in my math class, too."

"No, that must be my sister, Jessica."

"Gosh. You look exactly alike."

"That's because we're identical twins."

"That must be fun," Ginny Lu said, inching her way into the light. "I mean, playing jokes on people and stuff."

"Sometimes it is. And sometimes it's a problem. Especially if you have a sister who's as mischievous as mine!"

Ginny Lu flashed a big smile and Elizabeth thought that she looked quite pretty. Then she noticed what looked like a tiny wooden doll peeking out from the pocket of Ginny Lu's dress.

"That's neat. Where'd you get it?" Elizabeth asked, pointing at the doll.

"I whittled it," Ginny Lu replied. "Back home, I carve wooden dolls for the younger kids to play with. Then they dress 'em in scraps of material or whatever they can find." She held it up for Elizabeth to see.

"That's fantastic!" Elizabeth took the little figure and examined it. The body was carved simply but the eyes, nose, and lips were all clearly outlined in the wood. Even the strands of hair.

"You really like it?" Ginny Lu asked shyly.

"Of course I do," Elizabeth said. "I'm amazed that you could carve it all out of a single piece of wood."

"You can have it." Ginny Lu looked down at the ground and smiled.

"Why, thank you!"

Ginny Lu shrugged. "It just takes a little practice. I'm sure you could learn to do it in no time if you wanted to."

"Yes, but it wouldn't be as nice as this."

"My granddaddy taught me so I've had years of practice. Whittling is my favorite hobby." Ginny Lu put her hand over her mouth and whispered, "Or, I should say, second favorite." She stroked Snow White's neck. "Horses are my absolute number one favorite thing."

"Mine, too." Elizabeth patted the mare's nose. "I wish I had one."

"You don't have a horse?"

"No, I take riding lessons here and Ted—he's the stable boy and a great rider—Ted lets me ride his chestnut, Thunder."

"Boy, you're lucky." Ginny Lu buried her head into the white mare's neck. "I'd sure love it if Snow White's owner would let me ride her sometime." She looked back at Elizabeth and added, "After she's had her foal, of course. I wonder who her owner is."

Elizabeth hesitated. She didn't have the heart to tell Ginny Lu that Snow White belonged to her worst enemy in Sweet Valley.

She didn't have to. Just then a shrill voice cut through the air.

"Get away from my horse this instant!"

Ellen Riteman was standing at the door of the stall, her eyes flashing with anger.

"Snow White is . . . is *your* horse?" Ginny Lu asked in disbelief.

"Of course she's mine!" Ellen stamped her foot

on the ground. "And I am ordering you to get out of her stall this instant!"

"Ellen, why are you being so mean?" Elizabeth demanded. "Ginny Lu was just petting her."

Ellen ignored Elizabeth and stepped by her into the stall. "Come here, Snow White," she commanded shrilly.

The white mare's eyes widened with alarm. She darted backwards away from her mistress.

"Don't you disobey me!" Ellen yelled. "Bad girl!"

Snow White whinnied nervously, her nostrils flaring, and she beat against the stall with one of her hooves. In a flash Ginny Lu came between Ellen and the horse.

"It's all right, girl," Ginny Lu said. "Steady, now. No one's going to hurt you." She reached up and stroked the mare's neck and the horse calmed down.

"Good girl." Ginny Lu turned and walked slowly to the stall door. She unlatched the handle, taking care not to make any abrupt moves.

Ellen grabbed the edge of the lower door and swung it open wide. The sudden movement scared Snow White again and she reared up on her back legs.

"Easy, girl, easy," Ginny Lu said.

"I'll calm my own horse, if you don't mind," Ellen said.

"Well, everything you're doing seems to be scaring her," Ginny Lu said. "You have to keep a nice steady voice with animals and try not to make too many quick moves or—"

"This is my horse and I'll do what I want!" Ellen shouted. Elizabeth could tell that Ellen was getting embarrassed.

Ellen put her hands on her hips and faced Ginny Lu. "What are you doing here, anyway? This is a private club. Members only."

"Ginny Lu is here as my guest," Elizabeth said quickly. "She has every right to be here and I don't appreciate how you're treating her."

"Oh, you don't, eh?"

"No. You're not being very nice."

Ellen couldn't think of anything to say. She looked back and forth between the two girls, her face twisted with frustration and anger. "We'll just see about that!" Then she turned on her heel and marched off toward the office.

"Don't mind her," Elizabeth said, after Ellen had rounded the corner. "She's just upset. She loves her horse but she's been having trouble with her ever since Snow White got pregnant."

"Just the same," Ginny Lu muttered, "I think

I'll try and stay out of her way for a while." She looked over at Elizabeth and smiled. "Thanks for sticking up for me."

"Any time."

Ginny Lu looked back at Snow White and whistled softly. The mare's ears flipped up to attention and she ambled over to the stall door. Ginny Lu rubbed her face against the mare's neck and whispered, "Sure going to miss seeing you."

As Ginny Lu started to walk away, Elizabeth ran up beside her.

"Listen, maybe you'd like to come out here with me when I don't have my riding lesson. Then you could meet Ted and maybe ride Thunder."

Elizabeth lowered her voice and added, "And if you just happened to be near Snow White's stall and just happened to pet her, who'd ever know?"

A broad smile crossed Ginny Lu's freckled face. "Boy, I'd like that a lot!"

"OK, then. It's a deal!"

Six

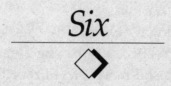

Crash!

Elizabeth flinched at the loud noise she heard as she walked through the front door. The sound was followed by a series of footsteps and then another loud crash. She sprinted up the stairs and followed the clamor to Jessica's bedroom. She found her sister standing in the middle of her room holding a large cardboard box filled with books. She dropped the carton on the floor with a thud.

"Jessica! What are you doing?"

"Thinking." Jessica spun in a quick circle, surveying her room, then marched through the bathroom straight into Elizabeth's room.

Elizabeth followed but stopped short at her doorway. "Jessica, call the police!" she gasped. "We've been robbed!"

The beautiful blue- and cream-colored room that she worked so diligently to keep tidy was in a shambles. The bed and desk were covered with clothes. Every drawer of her bureau was open, and worst of all, her favorite photo of the greatest race horse of all time, Man O'War, was gone.

"Calm down, Elizabeth," Jessica said. "We haven't been robbed. I'm having a garage sale." As Jessica talked, she moved to Elizabeth's closet and proceeded to throw more clothes onto the bed. "You see, I figure it's the fastest way to earn some money."

Elizabeth finally recovered enough to shout, "Don't touch another thing in that closet!"

The strength of her sister's voice stopped Jessica dead in her tracks. "What's the matter?"

"What's the matter?" Elizabeth repeated. "Look at my room! It's a mess."

"Oh, if *that's* all you're worried about," Jessica replied, "I promise I'll clean it up."

She started to move back to the closet but Elizabeth grabbed her arm first.

"Jess, why are you tearing my room apart?"

"I told you. I'm having a garage sale."

"Not with my things, you're not." Elizabeth

snatched up one of the dresses on the bed and carefully smoothed out the wrinkles.

"But, Elizabeth, you know you have the best clothes."

"That's because I take care of them and hang them up." Elizabeth carefully put her dresses and skirts back on their hangers. "And I still want to wear them."

"Please, Lizzie, I *have* to buy that tennis racket." Jessica put on her most pitiful voice.

"Then sell your own clothes."

"I don't have anything!" Jessica wailed. "I already looked."

Elizabeth marched back into her sister's room and dove into the closet. "You've got lots of clothes. Like this! You haven't worn this in a year." She held up a pink sweatshirt.

Jessica grabbed it out of her hands. "I couldn't sell that! I sometimes wear it when I get cold at the beach. Besides, it has a hole in it."

"The perfect reason to sell it."

Jessica looked absolutely aghast at the thought. "I don't want people to think my clothes have holes in them!"

"Jessica, that's what garage sales are for. You sell what you can't use anymore. And *all* of my clothes are still in use."

Elizabeth picked up the cardboard box and marched back to her room. "And one more thing," she yelled over her shoulder. "Sell your own books!"

"Oh, come on, Elizabeth. You've got twice as many as I have. You'll never miss them."

Elizabeth stared at her sister, dumbfounded. How could she explain that each book was a special treasure? Some of them she had read ten times.

"Hey, you two," a voice called from the top of the stairs in the hall. "What's going on in there?"

"Come on in, Mom!" Jessica called cheerily. "I was just helping Elizabeth weed out her closet."

"I would have thought it was the other way around," Mrs. Wakefield commented with a laugh.

"Jessica's room is next." Elizabeth gave her sister a mischievous smile.

"That's good to hear." Their mother stepped back into the hall. "Dinner will be ready in five minutes, girls."

"OK, Mom," Elizabeth replied. "We'll be right down."

While Elizabeth hung up her clothes and rearranged her drawers Jessica watched in mournful silence. When she'd finally put everything back in its place, Jessica released one more pitiful sigh.

"I guess the garage sale is off."

"I guess so."

As Jessica trudged wearily back out of the room, Elizabeth heard her mutter, "Back to the drawing board."

Later that evening, after Elizabeth had finished her homework, she strolled downstairs for a late night snack. Her mother was sitting at the dining room table, turning something over and over in her hands.

"Elizabeth, is this yours?" Her mother held up the little wooden doll that Ginny Lu had given her.

"Yes, the new girl in our class gave it to me. Her name is Ginny Lu. It must have fallen out of my pack. Isn't it pretty?"

"It's exquisite." Mrs. Wakefield held the carved figure up to the light. "A lovely example of Appalachian folk art."

"Really?" Elizabeth picked up an apple and sat down opposite her mother.

"Whittling dolls like these is almost a lost art," her mother explained. "Along with friendship quilts and authentic cornhusk dolls. I have a few clients who are collectors."

Mrs. Wakefield worked part-time for an interior design firm in Sweet Valley and sometimes had to scour the countryside for just the right antique or piece for a client.

"Wait till I tell Ginny Lu. She'll be thrilled," Elizabeth said.

"Well, you tell her that she is a true artist," her mother said.

Elizabeth took a bite of her apple and chewed it for a moment. An idea was brewing in her head. The Arts and Crafts Fair was the very next week and Mr. Clark had said they were looking for unusual displays. What if Ginny Lu entered her dolls in the show? That would be a perfect opportunity for her to make some new friends and build her confidence.

"Mom, you're a genius!" Elizabeth said suddenly.

"Thank you. But what did I do?"

"It's what you said. About folk art." Elizabeth took the doll out of her mother's hand. "I'm going to make sure that Ginny Lu Culpepper enters the Arts and Crafts Fair at Sweet Valley Middle School. I bet she'll even win!" She winked at the little doll and whispered, "That'll show Ellen Riteman a thing or two!"

At school the next day, Elizabeth couldn't wait to find Ginny Lu. But she did not see her at all until Mrs. Arnette's social studies class. Elizabeth tore a page out of her loose-leaf binder and hastily scribbled a note:

Ginny Lu,
Let's eat lunch together. I have a terrific idea
that's going to make you famous!!!

She drew a picture of a horse's head and signed
the note, "E.W." Then she added:

P.S. Mrs. Arnette looks grumpier than
usual. Maybe her bun is too tight.

Elizabeth carefully folded the note, caught
Ginny Lu's eye and then pretended to drop her pencil. They both bent over at the same time and passed
the note. Mrs. Arnette turned around just as they sat
back up in their desks and she eyed them suspi-
ciously.

As soon as the teacher turned back to the black-
board, Ginny Lu opened the note and read it. She
giggled out loud at the last part and then nodded a
quick "Yes!" to Elizabeth.

Later at lunch, Ginny Lu listened to Elizabeth's
proposal.

"I don't think it's such a great idea," she said
once Elizabeth had explained. "I mean, Ellen Riteman and her friends already make fun of me. Entering the fair might make things worse."

"No, it won't," Elizabeth insisted, "If you show your dolls in the Arts and Crafts Fair, people will get a chance to see how talented you are. And no one will make fun of you for that. Besides, I'll bet you'll win first prize!"

Ginny Lu blushed and looked down at her plate. "I suppose I could show them what Tennessee and the Smoky Mountains are like," Ginny Lu said. "Maybe even hang up a map and some pictures."

"You could do a whole display of the folk art and crafts from right around where you live."

"How 'bout some quilts. My mama's quilts win awards at the county fair all the time." She grinned proudly. "Aunt Barbara has one of her prize-winners."

"How about if you displayed other kinds of mountain crafts behind you and then let your special talent be whittling?" Elizabeth was growing more and more excited at the idea. "You know, you could even carve a doll as the judges walked around . . . kind of give a demonstration."

The idea was beginning to get Ginny Lu excited and her voice grew louder as she talked. Elizabeth noticed some kids at another table turn around and snicker but fortunately Ginny Lu didn't notice. "Oh, Elizabeth, my aunt would be so proud!" Ginny Lu clapped her hands together. "It might be just the thing to show her I can fit in."

"Hey, keep it down over there!"

Bruce Patman yelled over to them from two tables away. Then he mimicked Ginny Lu's accent so the whole cafeteria could hear. "You don't have to holler. We can hear you-all clear as day."

The sparkle disappeared from Ginny Lu's eyes and she stared down at her plate. Elizabeth could see that her cheeks were blazing pink with embarrassment.

"Bruce Patman, mind your own business," Elizabeth shouted back angrily. She picked up her tray and motioned to Ginny Lu. "Come on, let's go. We don't need to hang around these bores."

A grateful half-smile flickered across Ginny Lu's face. They dropped off their trays and then walked out of the cafeteria.

"Listen, Elizabeth," Ginny Lu said as the bell rang, "I'm still not sure this Arts and Crafts Fair is such a good idea—"

"Don't say no yet," Elizabeth broke in. "Come with me to the stables after school. We can talk about it more then."

Ginny Lu nodded. "Okay. But I don't think I'll change my mind."

"Just remember," Elizabeth said trying to prove a point, "guys like Bruce Patman don't have any special skills. You do."

"Now, hold on a minute!" Ginny Lu's eyes brightened. "If I remember right, Bruce makes a pretty good paper airplane."

Elizabeth burst out laughing, remembering how many times his paper planes had whizzed past her head in the hallway. "You're right about that, Ginny Lu!" Then she added, "But Bruce could never enter one in the fair."

Ginny Lu giggled and waved goodbye. "I'll think about it and see you later."

Seven

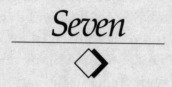

"PRIVATE PROPERTY—KEEP OUT"

Elizabeth read the newly painted sign on Snow White's stall out loud.

"I don't know what Ellen Riteman has against me," Ginny Lu said, shaking her head, "but she sure means business."

Elizabeth glanced around the empty stable, then whispered, "The sign says 'keep out,' but it doesn't say, 'don't feed the animals.'" She pulled a carrot out of her pack and handed it to Ginny Lu. "As long as you stay out of the stall, I guess you're OK."

"Thanks, Elizabeth." Ginny Lu took the carrot and held it over the stall door. She whistled softly into the dark shadows. "Come on, girl. I've got a special treat for you."

Snow White blinked her soft brown eyes and stepped up to the gate. The little mare shoved her muzzle playfully against Ginny Lu's shoulder, knocking her off balance.

"Whoa, girl, whoa!" Ginny Lu giggled with delight. "I would have come earlier but I promised my aunt I would try to stay in school for a full day."

Snow White let out a whinny and nudged her on the arm, trying to get at the carrot.

"Ooh, you're pushy today!" Ginny Lu laughed and opened her hand with the carrot. "There. Now you can have it."

Snow White ate the carrot and then prodded Ginny Lu's pockets with her nose, searching for another.

Elizabeth watched quietly, marveling at how good Ginny Lu was with horses. Around animals she became a different person, confident and sure of herself.

"I hate to rush you," Elizabeth said, "but my lesson starts in fifteen minutes and I need time to saddle Thunder and walk him to the ring."

Ginny Lu nodded. "Sure thing." She wrapped

her arms around the white mare's neck and whispered, " 'Bye, Snow White."

Moments later they were standing in Thunder's stall. While Ginny Lu fed the chestnut carrots and sugar cubes, Elizabeth slipped his bridle over his head. Then they walked him over to the tack room to get his saddle. Much to their dismay, Ellen Riteman was there.

"Just ignore her when we walk by," Elizabeth whispered to Ginny Lu. Both girls kept their eyes straight ahead as they passed. When they reached the tack room, Elizabeth handed the reins to Ginny Lu. "Hold Thunder while I get his saddle," Elizabeth said, hurrying into the building. Out of the corner of her eye, she noticed Ellen and her friends clustered in a circle, whispering.

Elizabeth pulled Thunder's saddle and blanket off their perch and ran back outside. Just as she was about to swing the saddle onto Thunder's back, Ginny Lu screamed, "Hold it! Don't put that on him, it's broken!"

Elizabeth dropped the saddle in midair. "What's wrong?"

"The saddle horn's fallen off!"

Hoots of laughter rang out behind her and Ginny Lu spun around. "What's so funny?"

Ellen Riteman was laughing so hard she could

barely get her words out. "Haven't you ever seen an English saddle before?"

Ginny Lu turned to Elizabeth, who whispered, "English saddles don't have saddle horns."

She hoped that Ginny Lu would calm down but it was too late. The fiery redhead put her hands on her hips and shouted, "Where I come from, we don't need saddles. We ride bareback. Saddles are for babies!"

Ellen stopped laughing and glared at Ginny Lu. "Babies, huh? We'll see about that."

Ellen pushed past Ginny Lu and ran into the tack room. When she reappeared she was carrying a western saddle. "We'll find out who's a baby around here!"

Ellen and her friends walked over to the far practice ring where a black mustang was tied to the main post.

"Uh-oh," Elizabeth said with a groan. "She's saddling up Midnight!"

"Who's Midnight?"

"Her father's mustang. Ellen never rides him because he's too wild. Ted's the only person who can handle him."

Ellen stepped cautiously toward the coal-black horse. After a few misses, Ellen managed to throw the saddle over his back. Then she turned to face Ginny Lu.

"OK, Little Miss Hick from the sticks," Ellen shouted. "I challenge you to ride Midnight!"

"Ginny Lu," Elizabeth whispered hurriedly, "I wouldn't if I were you."

"Oh, don't worry about me," Ginny Lu said quietly. "Back home I break ponies all the time."

She started to walk toward the ring and Elizabeth grabbed her arm. "But he's not a pony!"

"What's the matter?" Ellen taunted from across the ring. "You scared?"

Her friends started to chant in unison, "Scaredy-cat, scaredy-cat, Ginny Lu's a scaredy-cat!"

"You hear that?" Ginny Lu hissed. "Nobody calls me that!"

Before Elizabeth could stop her, Ginny Lu ran to the fence, hopped over and approached the horse.

"Come on, boy," she crooned, keeping her eyes glued to the mustang. "I'm not going to hurt you. Just let little old Ginny Lu mount you."

"Let's see if Ginny Lu, here, knows which end of the horse is the front!" Ellen jeered from the rail.

"You're going to be sorry you said that!" Ginny Lu yelled back.

Midnight sensed the tension in the air and flattened his ears back. He skittered back and forth, throwing his head up in jerky movements.

Ginny Lu kept her distance, all the while talking in a soothing tone, but Elizabeth could hear the nervous quiver in her voice. Suddenly Elizabeth became frightened that Ginny Lu might get hurt and she rushed to talk to Ellen.

"Ellen, this is getting dangerous. Don't let her ride Midnight."

"Nobody's forcing her to ride him," Ellen said calmly. "If she wants to admit she's a scaredy-cat, that's fine with me."

"Never!" Ginny Lu shouted, which caused the black horse to thrash at the ground with his front hoof. "There, there, boy," she purred, softening her voice. "Let's not get excited."

Elizabeth looked around, hoping that one of the teachers might be approaching the ring. But there were no adults in sight.

I know. I'll get Ted! she thought suddenly. *He'll make them stop.*

Elizabeth ran as fast as she could toward the main office of the stables.

Ginny Lu watched her go and her heart sank. Now she was completely alone. Her stomach felt like she had swallowed a hundred butterflies and they were all trying to get out at once.

Keep calm, she said to herself. *Don't let the horse know you're scared. Try to put Ellen out of your mind.*

Midnight stood still, eyeing her cautiously. Ginny Lu took a deep breath and walked up beside the black mustang. She could feel sweat on the horse's hide as she put a calm hand on his shoulder. His sides were heaving as he breathed in and out, snorting nervously.

Slowly, she reached up under his chin and grabbed the reins of the bridle. He lifted his head but didn't resist her. She untied him from the fence and started to walk the black horse around the ring in a circle. She hoped this would show him who was the boss.

"What are you going to do, walk him till someone comes to save you?" Ellen called from the side.

"I can ride this horse with my eyes closed!" Ginny Lu blurted out. She was so angry that she didn't take the time to steady Midnight before mounting him. She just stuck her left foot in the stirrup and swung her leg up in the air.

"Ginny Lu, look out!"

Elizabeth's voice carried down from the hill just as the saddle slipped sideways. Midnight reared up on his hind legs. Ginny Lu dropped the reins and threw her arms around the horse's neck, clawing at his mane for a grip. The useless saddle slipped off his back and fell onto the dirt.

The horse began to gallop around the ring, trying to shake her off. Ginny Lu was jostled so much, she thought her teeth would shake loose. She tried to kick her legs across the horse's back but it was all she could do to hang on.

Over the pounding of hooves she could hear a strange male voice shouting, "Whoa, boy, whoa!" Suddenly the mustang came to an abrupt stop. Ginny Lu felt her body jerk forward over his head. Then the whole world turned upside down.

She hit the ground with a thunk. The impact knocked the breath out of her and she realized she couldn't move. The arena was completely silent except for the sound of Midnight's hooves, as he galloped away from her.

"Ginny Lu, are you hurt?"

Ginny Lu blinked at Elizabeth who was kneeling beside her. The painful jolt had brought tears to her eyes. Her chin quivered as she mumbled gruffly, "Just my pride."

Elizabeth helped her to her feet and Ginny Lu winced. "My pride and my tailbone," she added, rubbing it.

"Well, if it makes you feel any better," Elizabeth

said, holding her friend by the elbow, "you're the first one of us ever even to *try* to ride Midnight!"

"I could've, too, if that saddle had been buckled."

Elizabeth's eyes grew wide with horror. "You mean Ellen didn't cinch it?"

As if in answer, Ted's angry voice cut through the air. "Ellen Riteman, that was one of the most irresponsible things I have ever seen! That girl could have been seriously hurt. I'm going to make sure your father hears about this!"

As Ted strode out of the ring, Ellen hurried after him. "Don't tell him, Ted, please!"

"See, it's Ellen who's the big baby," Elizabeth whispered. "You don't need to prove a thing to her."

"Yes, I do," Ginny Lu said quietly. "I want her to know I'm as good as she is."

"Well, you're not going to prove that by breaking your neck."

"That's for sure." Ginny Lu kicked at the dirt. "But what else can I do?"

This was the chance Elizabeth had been waiting for. "Well, one way you can prove yourself is to enter the Arts and Crafts Fair."

Ginny Lu shook her head so hard, her braids lashed back and forth. "No way!"

Elizabeth shrugged. "I just thought that since Ellen was entering the contest . . . "

"She's entering?" Ginny Lu interrupted.

Elizabeth nodded. "She said she's going to enter her horse drawings."

"Horse drawings!" Ginny Lu repeated. "Why, I can do better than that!"

"Then why don't you?"

"Maybe I will." Ginny Lu put her hands on her hips. "Maybe I'll show Ellen and some of those kids that you don't mess around with a girl from Tennessee!"

"Right!" Elizabeth encouraged her.

"I *will* enter that contest," Ginny Lu announced. "And maybe I'll even win!"

"That's the spirit!"

Elizabeth was answered by a loud whinny from in front of the tack room.

"Come on!" she said. "Poor old Thunder has been tied up forever and he knows I've got another carrot for him."

Ginny Lu followed Elizabeth back to the tack room with a definite bounce in her step. Suddenly, beating Ellen Riteman was the most important thing in her life!

Eight

◇

"It's now or never," Jessica said, as she stood outside her brother's door on Saturday morning. She hated asking Steven for a favor but time was running out. She knew her father was going to be playing tennis soon and she desperately needed the money to replace his racket. Steven was her last hope.

Jessica put on her sweetest smile and tapped gently on his door.

"Who is it?" a voice mumbled from inside.

"It's Jess. Can I talk to you a second?"

"What's the password?"

"I'm serious, Steven." Jessica usually would

have played along with her brother, but today she didn't have the time. "I have to talk to you."

"So?"

"So, open your door!" She could feel her temper starting to go.

Steven put on his Dracula accent. "Nobody enters the chambers of Count Wakefield unless they speak the secret password!"

"Steven, I don't have time to play games. You open this door this minute!"

"Open it yourself," Steven drawled in his normal voice. "It's not locked."

Jessica burst through the door. Steven looked up, startled. He had his ten-speed bicycle turned upside down on newspapers and the gears were spread out over the floor. The greasy chain hung from his hands. "Jess, what's so important that you have to kick down my door?" he asked.

Jessica was about to reply sarcastically when she remembered her mission. She quietly worked her way across the room and sat on his bed. Taking a moment to regain her composure, she began the little speech she'd practiced all afternoon.

"Steven, I've been thinking—"

"That's something new!" He grinned at her.

"Very funny. Now that you're a star on the bas-

ketball team, I'll bet keeping up with your school-
work is really hard for you."

"It sure is." Steven motioned for her to hand
him the socket wrench.

Jessica gave it to him and then tried to find some
place to wipe the grease that had gotten on her hand.

"And with all that basketball practice and homework, it must be extra hard keeping up with your
household chores."

"It's a pain." He nodded. "I'm already two
weeks behind on cleaning the upstairs floors and
this morning Dad asked me to clean out the garage."

Jessica's eyes sparkled. That was just what she
wanted to hear.

"Well, I've got a little proposition to make that
might just help you out."

Her brother stopped working and eyed her sus-
piciously. Jessica added quickly, "And it will help
me, too."

"That's more like the Jessica I know."

"Here it is," Jessica began. "I'll do your household chores for you if you'll pay me your weekly
allowance."

"Then what am I going to do for money?"

Jessica hadn't thought about that. She bit her lip
thoughtfully. "Okay, you can keep part of your allowance. Ten percent."

"Half."

"Half?" she blurted out. "While I'm doing all the work?"

"If you really want to help me out—" Steven smiled mischievously, "—then that's the deal."

"Steven! Sometimes you make me so mad!" Jessica knew he had her and there was nothing she could do about it.

"I think you should get started right away," Steven declared. He pulled a broom and dustpan from under his bed and handed them to Jessica. "Mom said she needed the hall swept and dusted. Pronto."

Jessica grabbed the broom and briefly thought about using it on her brother's head.

"Temper, temper!" he cautioned with a sly grin, one hand held up in protest. "Or the deal is off.

"Oh, and Jessica?"

She turned to look at him from the doorway. "Yes?"

"Don't tell Mom and Dad about our little plan. I don't think they'd be too keen about it. We'll just pretend you're helping me out 'cause you like me so much."

"You make me sick!" Jessica slammed the door to block out his laughter but she could hear him all the way down the hall to her room.

* * *

By Friday, Jessica was ready to quit. But she forced herself to hold out until she had gotten Steven's money. That night after dinner Mrs. Wakefield gave them their allowances.

"I just want you to know how pleased we are with you three this week," Mrs. Wakefield said as they sat around the dining room table. "And," she added, "Steven, I am simply amazed. For once, you did everything we asked of you."

Steven flashed a smile that stretched from ear to ear.

"Of course, I know you couldn't have done it without your helper," she said, turning toward Jessica. "Jessica, your father and I both noticed how thoughtful you've been to your brother this week and we want you to know we appreciate it."

Mrs. Wakefield looked back at Steven and continued, "Steven, we hope you will be as considerate toward your sister."

"Sure, Mom," Steven replied solemnly.

"And for setting such a good example, Jessica, your father and I have decided to give you a little bonus with your allowance this week."

"What!" Steven almost leaped out of his seat. "That's not fair!"

"Steven, how can you say that?" Mrs. Wakefield

asked. "Jessica has worked so hard to help you."

"But—"

"I saw her out there, hauling boxes around the garage, while you were shooting baskets with your friends."

"But—"

"And taking out the garbage while you and Joe Howell played video games in the den," Mr. Wakefield added.

Steven sunk into a stony silence. Mrs. Wakefield looked at him sternly and said, "I think you owe Jessica an apology."

He started to object again but the look on his mother's face made Steven think better of it. When he turned to face his sister, Jessica was wearing her most angelic expression.

"I'm sorry, Jessica," he said between clenched teeth.

As Elizabeth watched the exchange between her sister and brother, a light went on in her head. *Of course!* she thought. *Jessica's been doing Steven's chores to get his allowance to pay for the tennis racket! And now she's doubly rewarded for it by Mom and Dad.*

Mr. and Mrs. Wakefield left the dining room and Jessica waited only a moment before she held out her hand. "OK, Steven, pay up!"

Steven shot her his most withering look. Grumbling the whole time, he counted out half of his allowance and dropped it into her hand. "I still don't think it's fair."

At that moment, the doorbell rang, interrupting their squabbling, and Elizabeth ran to answer it.

Someone stood on their front porch, balancing a big cardboard box in each arm. Elizabeth could barely make out the top of a red head.

"Hi," a voice drawled from behind the boxes. "It's me, Ginny Lu. I brought the dolls and stuff for the fair."

Elizabeth grabbed one of the boxes and held open the door for Ginny Lu. She led her up the stairs, pausing just long enough to call, "Mom, Ginny Lu is here."

"I'll be right there."

"I thought my mother might be able to give us some tips on setting up the display."

"Great idea!" said Ginny Lu. At Elizabeth's bedroom doorway, Ginny Lu stopped and whistled. "Boy, your room sure is pretty."

"Thank you." Elizabeth smiled and set the box on her bed. Then she reached for a yellow piece of paper she had laid on her desk.

"I picked up the rules for the contest from Mr. Clark's office. Each contestant gets a six-foot-wide booth with a table."

"That should be plenty of room to show Mama's quilt and her homemade preserves."

Both girls sat on the bed and examined the rules for the contest. Ginny Lu pointed to the last line on the page.

"It says we each get five minutes with the judges. What'll I say?"

"You can use that time for anything. I think you should demonstrate how you whittle these." Elizabeth reached into the cardboard box and carefully removed the dolls.

Each was dressed like a pioneer woman, in a long calico dress and matching bonnet, and stood about eight inches high. Ginny Lu had whittled each face and even carved delicate little hands for each of the dolls.

"These are beautiful, Ginny Lu. Each one is so different."

"Some of them I had already made in Stony Gap but these three I whittled here." She pointed to the ones carved from pine. "Aunt Barbara helped me make the dresses."

"Well, I think they are exquisite," Mrs. Wakefield declared from the doorway. "If I were a judge, you'd have my vote for first place!"

"Why, thank you, ma'am," Ginny Lu said with an excited giggle.

Elizabeth's mother held up one of the dolls and examined it closely. "You know, dolls like these are very rare. They can sell for, oh, twenty-five dollars apiece in craft stores."

Jessica, who was sweeping the hall outside her sister's room, froze at her mother's words.

"Twenty-five dollars!" she gasped. Her mind started clicking away like an adding machine. Selling just two of those dolls could pay for the tennis racket! If she could talk Ginny Lu into letting her show her dolls to some of the stores—why, they could be rich! Of course, she would have to convince Ginny Lu that she should be her partner. But that didn't worry Jessica. Once she turned on her famous charm, Ginny Lu Culpepper would be begging her to be her business manager.

Jessica marched straight down the hall to Steven's room. She knocked three times on his door and sang, "Yoo-hoo! Count Wakefield!"

A voice inside responded in a Dracula accent. "What's the password?"

Jessica opened the door and tossed the broom at her brother. "Do your own dirty work," she snapped.

Then she carefully shut Steven's door and giggled all the way back to her room.

Nine

◇

Saturday morning at exactly ten o'clock, the doors of the gym at Sweet Valley Middle School swung open and crowds of people began pouring inside.

A long banner announcing, "THE TENTH ANNUAL ARTS AND CRAFTS FAIR," fluttered gaily over their heads.

Ginny Lu had been assigned a booth in one of the corners of the room. Sizing up the situation, Elizabeth and Ginny Lu decided to take advantage of the joining walls and decorate the corner to look like an old-fashioned country kitchen.

They stocked the corner shelves with brightly labeled jars of Mrs. Culpepper's fruit preserves. On the other wall they hung her prizewinning quilt, with a sign beneath it that read, "Wedding Ring Pattern." An oak butter churn Mrs. Wakefield had borrowed from an antique store sat in front of the quilt.

"Is everything ready?" Ginny Lu asked, nervously eyeing the approaching crowd. She smoothed her gingham skirt and pulled at the hem of the hand-embroidered apron she wore.

"I think so." Elizabeth put the final touches on the booth's sign. Then she sat back and read proudly, "Folk Art from the Great Smoky Mountains. Ginny Lu Culpepper, Sixth Grade."

Ginny Lu sat on a wooden stool next to the churn, pulled out her jackknife and a piece of soft pine, and started whittling.

Elizabeth flicked on a cassette recorder hidden behind the table and a spirited mountain jig began to play softly. It gave the booth just the right touch.

"Well, you're all set," Elizabeth announced. "I'm going to check out the competition. I'll be back."

Elizabeth strolled up the aisle. There were the usual exhibits—macraméd hangings and planters, knit items, crocheted blankets and afghans, jewelry and stained-glass ornaments. Elizabeth hurried back. She couldn't wait to report to Ginny Lu.

"I just took a look at the other entries," she announced with a grin, "and yours is by far the most original!"

Ginny Lu's eyes shone. "I sure hope you're right!"

While they were talking, Charlie Cashman and Jerry McAllister appeared and stood off at a distance, watching Ginny Lu whittle. They stared at her hands, absolutely fascinated.

Finally Jerry McAllister, who considered himself a pretty good carpenter, spoke up.

"What are you making?"

"This is what's known as a whimmy diddle," she explained. Both boys laughed and Ginny Lu said, "I know it's a funny name but that's all I've ever heard it called."

"What's it do?" Charlie asked, stepping closer to the table.

"See this?" Ginny Lu held up a little hand-carved propeller with a tiny hole in the center. They both nodded.

"I'm going to attach this to the end of this stick with a finishing nail." She tacked the nail in with a hammer and spun the propeller to see that it turned freely. "Then, when I rub a stick over these notches, the propeller will spin by itself."

"No kidding?" Jerry said, joining Charlie to get

a closer look. A few other sixth graders stopped at Ginny Lu's booth, curious to see what was going on.

"Some people call it a gee-haw whimmy diddle," Ginny Lu went on, warming to her audience.

"Gee-haw?" Charlie repeated. "What's that mean?"

"Gee and haw are commands you give to a horse to make 'em go right or left." She held up the toy. "This is a gee-haw whimmy diddle because you can make the propeller go to the right or left, depending on how you hold the stick."

She demonstrated the whimmy diddle and little gasps of delight came from the crowd. Ginny Lu handed the toy to Charlie. "Here, you try it."

"Where'd you learn that?" Jerry asked, as Charlie rubbed the stick and laughed delightedly when the propeller started to spin.

"My granddaddy taught me," Ginny Lu said. "But everyone in Stony Gap knows how to make them."

"Could you teach us?" Charlie asked. A couple of other boys that had joined them chorused, "Yeah, me, too!"

"Sure. There really isn't much to it. While I'm at it, I could teach you how to make smoke grinders, which are like spinning tops."

"That would be cool!" Jerry said.

As Elizabeth watched Ginny Lu demonstrate the toys, she couldn't help feeling proud. The kids from Sweet Valley were discovering a whole new side to the redheaded girl from Tennessee.

The tape ran out and Elizabeth went to flip over the cassette. As she punched the start button she noticed the judges starting to make their rounds.

There were four judges, one from each of the competing middle schools. Mr. Sweeney, her art teacher, was representing Sweet Valley Middle School. At each display they examined the entries carefully and then chatted for a few minutes with the contestant.

The crowd around Ginny Lu was getting bigger by the second. More and more of the students were coming over to watch. Out of the corner of her eye, Elizabeth noticed Ellen Riteman and two of her friends leave their booths to join the crowd. At the same moment, the judges reached Ginny Lu's exhibit and began to take notes.

Elizabeth raised her hand and whispered, "Go!"

Ginny Lu took a deep breath and began to recite a poem she had rehearsed at Elizabeth's house the night before. They had decided that that would be the crowning touch for her exhibit. It was about a young boy and his father, who lived all alone in the mountains. Each night the father would take down his fiddle and play until dawn as he practiced for a big contest.

Ginny Lu's voice played with the rhythm of the poem. She made it sound like a fiddle going faster and faster.

He fiddled in the meadow, fiddled in the glen;
Fiddled over Piney Top and fiddled home again.

By this time some of the audience had begun to clap in time with the words. Elizabeth noted with delight that even the judges were tapping their toes. Then Elizabeth tuned back into Ginny Lu.

So he took his daddy's fiddle,
    and the young boy played and played,
And while the bow sawed back and forth,
    the coonhounds bayed and bayed!

A loud snickering erupted from the back of the audience. Elizabeth spun around to see Ellen Riteman and her friends trying to stifle their giggles behind their hands. Nearby Bruce Patman and Joe Howell let out a yowl like a hound dog.

Ginny Lu blushed and almost forgot her next

line. But she recovered and bravely kept on with her story. She told how the young boy won the contest for his father and brought the ribbon back home. When she came to the final verse, with its chorus about the coonhounds, Ginny Lu shut her eyes.

> He laid the bright blue ribbon,
>   on his daddy's fresh dug grave;
> Then taking up his bow in hand,
>   the young boy played and played;
> And while he made that fiddle sing—

Ginny Lu paused and looked grimly in Ellen's direction. She never said the last line. Ellen and her friends finished it for her.

> The coonhounds bayed and bayed!

Then, to Ginny Lu's horror, the rest of the crowd shouted the line again.

> And the coonhounds bayed and bayed!

Ginny Lu stumbled off the stool, catching her foot and nearly tripping. She searched frantically for a way out of the gym. Then spotting the exit sign, she shoved the table away from the wall, toppling her dolls, and ran as fast as she could.

She felt like she could hardly breathe. The total humiliation of it all pounded in her head like a freight train. The only sound she was aware of was her own voice crying, "Let me out of here!"

Ten

◇

Elizabeth was frantic. She'd spent the last hour looking all over the school grounds for Ginny Lu but her
friend was nowhere to be found.

She was exhausted and her feet hurt. Just as she
was about to give up, Elizabeth spotted her sister
entering the gym and she rushed to join her.

"Jess, I'm so glad you're here! Have you seen
Ginny Lu?"

Jessica shook her head. "No. That's why I came.
I have some great news. Mom gave me a list of shops
she thought would be interested in Ginny Lu's dolls
and I went to see them this morning. The first shop

wasn't interested, but the second said yes! They'll pay twenty-five dollars apiece for the dolls. Isn't that great!"

"Oh, Jess, that's terrific!" Elizabeth replied.

"I can't wait to tell Ginny Lu," Jessica said.

"If we could only find her."

"What do you mean?" For the first time since her arrival Jessica noticed her sister's gloomy look. "What's wrong, Elizabeth?"

"Ellen Riteman and a few other kids made fun of Ginny Lu during her poem."

"Oh, no! Did it ruin her chances for winning?"

Elizabeth shook her head. "I don't think so but it sure upset Ginny Lu. She disappeared before the judges could talk to her. Jess, I feel responsible. I'm the one who talked her into entering this contest."

She slumped down onto some bleachers and Jessica sat down beside her. "Don't worry, Lizzie. I'm sure she'll turn up."

"I hope you're right." Elizabeth forced herself to smile.

They were distracted by a crackling noise from the loudspeakers. A tall man in a blue blazer was standing by a microphone at the front of the room.

"Welcome, everyone. It's good to see such a large crowd here on this beautiful Saturday afternoon. I have to say, I think the handiwork displayed this year is the best we've ever had. Let's hear it for all the participants."

There was a loud round of applause from the crowd. Then the man explained the rules for judging. Jessica and Elizabeth listened as they continued to search the crowd for any sign of Ginny Lu.

"Where do you think she could have gone?" Jessica whispered.

"I checked all around the school grounds and in the bathrooms."

"Maybe she's with her aunt."

Elizabeth shook her head. "No, I talked to Mrs. Waldron a little while ago and she couldn't find her either."

The man on the stage held up an envelope and announced, "It looks like the judges have made their decisions."

Jessica stood up with her hands on her hips. "Boy, Ginny Lu must have felt really terrible. She didn't even wait around to hear the winners."

"Jess, I'm really worried about her." Elizabeth grasped her sister's arm and pulled herself to her feet. "I'm going to go look for her."

"Okay. I'll wait here in case she decides to come back."

"Great. I'll try her house first."

"And if she doesn't come back here, I'm going to Ellen Riteman's house," Jessica announced.

Elizabeth's eyes widened in surprise and Jessica explained, "I'm going to tell Ellen to be nice to Ginny Lu—or else!"

Elizabeth grinned and set off for the nearest exit.

"I'm going home and never, ever, coming back to this awful place again!"

Ginny Lu threw her suitcase on top of the bedspread and filled it with her few belongings. Then she carried it downstairs to the sitting room and sat down at her aunt's desk. She opened a drawer and pulled out a slip of paper and a pen. After a moment's thought, she wrote:

Dear Aunt Barbara,

You've probably heard how I placed last at the fair and made a laughingstock out of myself and our whole family. Well, I'm not going to embarrass you anymore. I'm going home.

By the time you get this, I will be on my way to Stony Gap. I'm sorry for all the trouble I've been. I guess I just can't fit in with the life out here. Thanks for everything.

Love, your niece,
Ginny Lu Culpepper

As she folded the note and propped it on the desk, Ginny Lu's eyes filled with tears. She realized that there were some things she was going to miss. She loved her Aunt Barbara and her home. She liked having a room all to herself. And even though Ellen Riteman and Lila Fowler had been so awful to her, Elizabeth Wakefield and her friends were kind.

But even so, she thought, she didn't fit in at Sweet Valley and she never would. The only real friend she had made was a horse.

Just thinking about the pretty Arabian mare made Ginny Lu's heart ache. In the quiet refuge of the stall she had often poured out her heart, telling the horse all about the loneliness and frustration she felt in Sweet Valley. When she looked into the mare's warm brown eyes, Ginny Lu knew for certain that Snow White was the only creature who really understood her. She couldn't leave town without saying goodbye to her only friend. Ellen Riteman or no Ellen Riteman, she had to see the little mare one more time.

She took one last look around the big friendly house and then closed the door behind her.

I'd better follow the side roads out to the stables, she thought, *just in case Aunt Barbara finds my note and comes looking for me.*

She picked up her suitcase and hurried toward Carson Stables for a final visit with Snow White.

When Mrs. Waldron answered Elizabeth's knock on her door, she was holding Ginny Lu's note in her hand. She looked as though she had been crying.

"Poor Ginny Lu. I just feel terrible. I promised her mother that I would take care of her—and look what happened!"

"It's not your fault, Mrs. Waldron. I'm sure we'll find her."

"I just don't know where to look," Mrs. Waldron said, walking to the phone in the hall. "I guess I'll call the highway patrol, and check the bus station and airport."

As Elizabeth watched Mrs. Waldron leaf through the phone book, she got an inspiration.

"Before you make those calls, Mrs. Waldron, I think there's one place we should look first."

"Where?"

"Carson Stables."

Mrs. Waldron gave her a confused look and Elizabeth explained, "You see, there's this pretty white mare that Ginny Lu is crazy about. And the horse is in foal and really won't let anyone but Ginny Lu get near her. Anyway, Ginny Lu is very attached to that horse. I think we should check there."

"Oh." Mrs. Waldron nodded her head. "Well, let's go see. I just hope we're not too late."

Eleven

◇

Ginny Lu leaned against the sign for Carson Stables and tried to catch her breath. She hid her suitcase behind one of the white fence posts, then hurried up the lane to the stables.

Because it was Saturday, most of the horses were out of their stalls. Both practice rings were filled with classes in progress. She could see groups of riders dotting the hillside.

Ginny Lu tiptoed down the row of stalls, keeping a careful watch for unexpected visitors. The last person she wanted to run into was Ellen Riteman.

A loud whinny cut through the air and a male

voice answered it. "Easy, girl, you're going to be all right. That a girl, easy!"

Ginny Lu's heart started to pound. It was Ted and his voice was coming from Snow White's stall. Something was wrong with the little mare! She ran to the open door and gasped in horror.

Snow White was facing the door, panting heavily. Ted stood just inside the door, doing his best to approach the mare. But every time he got close, her nostrils flared and the whites of her eyes showed. Her ears were lying flat against her head, a sure sign that she was afraid.

Then she noticed something was different. "Snow White's had her foal!"

Lying motionless in the hay a few feet from Snow White was a tiny brown colt, looking scruffy and very groggy.

"That's right," Ted said. "But she wasn't due for another couple of weeks."

"Is the colt all right?"

"I can't tell," Ted replied.

Ginny Lu leaned across the stable door. "Judging by the looks of that little fella, he should have been on his feet long ago. Why, his fur is already dry from where his mama cleaned him."

Ted nodded. "I found them about forty-five minutes ago and she had just given birth."

"Forty-five minutes ago?" A horrible fear gripped Ginny Lu. "That little horse is premature. If he doesn't start nursing soon, he'll die!"

"But Snow White won't let me get near him. If we don't help him stand up and get to his mother soon, I don't know what will happen." A note of panic had crept into Ted's voice.

Ginny Lu tried to keep her own voice calm as she asked, "Did you call a vet?"

"Dr. Keating's on an emergency. Her office said she'll get here as soon as she can. In the meantime, I called the Ritemans."

Just the thought of Ellen made Ginny Lu's stomach tighten in knots. Then a feeble whinny came from the little foal. He lifted his head weakly and looked right at Ginny Lu.

"He wants me to help him!" she cried out. Without a moment's hesitation, Ginny Lu pushed back the door and stepped into the stall.

"Be careful!" Ted warned. "She might hurt you."

"Aw, Snow White knows me," Ginny Lu said soothingly. "Don't you, girl?"

The mare's eyes flickered forward at the sound of Ginny Lu's voice. She watched Ginny Lu inch up beside her but didn't respond. "There, there."

Slowly Ginny Lu reached out her hand and gently rubbed the white mare's neck. The horse visibly relaxed. She snorted softly and pressed her head into Ginny Lu's hand.

"That's amazing," Ted said.

Ginny Lu scratched Snow White behind the ears and intently studied the tiny foal.

"I'm going to see if Snow White will let me get close to the foal," she whispered. She gave Snow White another reassuring pat and slowly eased onto her knees next to the colt.

"How do you know so much about horses?" Ted asked.

"I help my daddy all the time back home in Tennessee. We have a couple of horses, one old mule and, of course, I've watched a lot of animals being born."

She gently rubbed the little foal's head. "He looks OK, Ted. I just think he wasn't quite strong enough to get out in the world yet."

Snow White lowered her head next to Ginny Lu and nudged the little colt, encouraging him to stand.

"Your mama wants you to get up and I think you'd better do what she wants." Ginny Lu wrapped her arms around the foal and lifted him to his feet. His knees buckled immediately but she held him tight.

Suddenly, Ginny Lu was startled by an earsplitting shriek that came from the stable door.

"Get away from my horse!"

Ellen Riteman stood framed against the stall door. Her hair was mussed and her face bright red from running. Jessica was right behind her, out of breath, too.

"Ellen, you promised to be nice," Jessica managed to say.

"But I didn't promise to let her hurt my horse!" Ellen glared back at Ginny Lu. "Get out of there this instant!"

Snow White tossed her head nervously at all the commotion and Ginny Lu nearly dropped the colt.

"Calm down, Ellen." Ted put his hand on her arm. "She's not hurting your horse. Ginny Lu is the only person Snow White will let get near her colt."

"But what's she doing to him?" Ellen sounded like she was going to cry.

"She's trying to save his life."

"I think Dr. Keating should do that, not her."

"I called the vet and she'll be here soon—but we can't wait that long. That foal was premature and he's too weak to stand by himself. If he doesn't get to his mother, he could die."

"What?" Ellen turned completely white. "Oh, no!"

Ginny Lu spoke up, keeping her attention focused on the foal all the time. "Every second we waste, this little fella gets weaker and weaker. It's important he gets his mama's milk right now."

Ted nodded grimly. "She's right, Ellen."

"I don't know what to do!" Ellen looked back and forth between Ted and Ginny Lu. Finally she turned to Jessica for advice.

"You've got to trust Ginny Lu and Ted," Jessica said quietly. "I think they know more than we do."

Ellen hesitated. She ran her hand through her hair several times. Finally she nodded. "OK. But be careful!"

They held their breath as Ginny Lu carefully lifted and carried the colt over to his mother. When she set him down his legs wobbled and he nearly lost his balance but after a few tries and with help from Ginny Lu he managed to stay on his feet.

Ginny Lu kept one arm around him, to steady him, then gently guided his muzzle to his mother's side.

"All right!" Ted whispered, sounding relieved.

No one spoke as they watched the newborn foal with his mother. His tiny brush of a tail twitched eagerly as he nursed.

Jessica's eyes glowed. "He's beautiful!"

Ellen squeezed Jessica's hand and nodded. "Isn't he?"

* * *

By the time Elizabeth and Mrs. Waldron arrived, Dr. Keating had everything under control.

"You should be very proud of your niece, Mrs. Waldron," the veterinarian said, once they had all been introduced. "Her quick thinking probably saved this little foal's life."

"It was nothing," Ginny Lu mumbled. Elizabeth grinned as she saw her friend's face turn beet-red.

Suddenly Ellen Riteman, who hadn't said a word, piped up. "The doctor's right. Ginny Lu was the only one of us who knew what to do."

They all looked at Ellen in surprise. A wide smile crept across Ginny Lu's face. "Well, you were the one who let me help."

Ellen responded with a genuine grin. Then she dropped her head and said, "I think I, uh . . . owe you an apology for a couple of things. I haven't been very nice or fair to you. Maybe I can make it up somehow."

"You don't have to do that."

"Well, I just thought that, since Snow White likes you so much, and you helped with the birth, and all . . ." Ellen lifted her head and smiled at Ginny Lu. "Maybe you should name the colt."

The two girls looked at each other without speaking. "I'd like that," Ginny Lu finally said. "And I know just the perfect name for him—Sooner.

Because he decided he'd rather get here sooner than later. And now that he's here, he's decided he'd sooner stay."

Everyone laughed. Then Mrs. Waldron asked, "How about you, Ginny Lu? Which would you rather do? Go or stay?"

"What?" Jessica exclaimed. "You're not thinking of leaving, are you? You can't! I found a shop that wants to buy your dolls. And I have it all figured out. We'll each take half."

"Half?" Elizabeth repeated, raising one eyebrow.

Jessica caught her sister's glare and said guiltily, "OK, OK, ten percent. I can still buy the tennis racket and have money left over."

Ginny Lu looked from face to face, thoroughly confused. "Why would anyone want to buy my dolls?"

"Because they're beautiful," Elizabeth said.

Ginny Lu tugged at one of her braids and made a face. "I'll bet the judges at the fair didn't think so."

"Judges!" Jessica yelled, then quickly covered her mouth, not wanting to disturb Snow White and her foal. "I knew there was something I had to tell you!"

Everyone turned to look at Jessica. "I forgot to

tell you the most important news of all. You won, Ginny Lu!"

"I did?" Ginny Lu looked completely amazed.

"You won the biggest prize of all, 'Best of Show' at the entire Arts and Crafts Fair!"

Mrs. Waldron put her arms around her niece and hugged her tightly. "Congratulations, honey. You deserved it."

"Boy, I think I need to sit down." Ginny Lu looked as wobbly as the new foal. "So many good things are happening at once."

"You still haven't answered my question," her aunt persisted. "Are you going, or staying?"

This time Ellen spoke up. "You can't go now. Who's going to help me with Snow White and Sooner?"

"Besides," Elizabeth said softly, "I'd miss you a lot."

"Me, too!" Jessica echoed.

They looked at her expectantly, waiting for her answer. Ginny Lu smiled up at her aunt and then over at the Wakefield twins.

"Well, maybe I'll stick around. At least till Sooner is strong enough to gallop around with his mama."

She was answered by a loud whinny from inside the stall.

Jessica giggled. "Snow White thinks it's a good idea."

"And so do the rest of us," Elizabeth added.

Twelve

◇

On Monday morning Elizabeth dashed out of her classroom as soon as the bell rang. The whole school was buzzing with excitement. Mr. Clark had made an announcement over the public address system. A special assembly was to be held in the auditorium during third period.

"What do you think it's all about?" Amy Sutton asked, as she and Nora Mercandy came up beside Elizabeth.

"I wish I knew."

Nora looked both ways slyly and whispered, "I heard from Mrs. Knight in the office that they're planning a big celebration."

"What for?" Amy asked.

Nora shrugged. "Something about a school anniversary or something."

"That's right!" Elizabeth exclaimed. "I completely forgot. Remember, Mr. Clark told us about the anniversary once before, and Mr. Bowman suggested we make it the theme of the next issue of *The Sweet Valley Sixers*."

They were interrupted by Jessica's shouting from down the hall. "Guess what?" Jessica shouted again as she made her way closer to Elizabeth. "Ginny Lu dropped off her dolls at the folk art shop this morning. The man paid her in cash for all of them!"

"That's wonderful!" Elizabeth replied.

"She gave me my share just before first period." Jessica caught the questioning look in her twin's eye and added hastily, "Ten percent agent's fee. That's *all*."

Elizabeth lowered her voice and added, "So what about the . . . you-know-what?"

Jessica beamed at her. "I'm picking it up after school. It'll be in the closet before Dad gets home from work. And I can pay you back now, too, Lizzie."

"I don't understand," Amy interrupted. "What are you talking about?"

"It's a long story," Elizabeth replied.

Jessica smiled at her sister. "But one with a happy ending!"

Jessica left her twin and continued down the hall until she found Tamara Chase and some of the other Unicorns standing beside the water fountain. As Jessica approached, Lila stepped away from the others and pulled Jessica to the side of the building.

"Listen," she whispered intently. "I found out what the assembly is all about."

"How'd you—?"

"Never mind how," Lila interrupted. "Just listen."

Jessica nodded excitedly. She could tell that Lila was onto something big.

"Since this is the twenty-fifth anniversary of Sweet Valley Middle School," Lila said, "they're planning something really special to celebrate."

"What is it?"

Lila took a deep breath, then said, "A time capsule."

Jessica looked confused. "A what?"

"A time capsule," Lila repeated. "You take articles from today, like newspapers and records, bury them in the ground, and then people dig them up years from now."

"So?"

"So, there's going to be a contest. Whoever wins will get their pictures put in the time capsule, which won't be opened for twenty-five years."

"You mean, people will know all about the winners when they open the capsule again?"

Lila nodded. "They'll be famous forever."

"Wow!" Jessica's mind reeled at the thought of being famous way off in the future. "What are the rules?"

"I don't know. That's what the assembly's about," Lila replied.

"I have to win that contest," Jessica declared softly.

"*We* have to win," Lila corrected her. "This is a chance for the whole world to know, forever and ever, that the Unicorns were the smartest and most popular girls at school."

Jessica nodded solemnly. "Of course."

The bell rang and the two girls headed for the auditorium. As she stepped through the double doors, a determined smile crept over Jessica's face.

I'm going to win that contest, she thought. *No matter what it takes!*

Find out if Jessica will become a Sweet Valley legend in Sweet Valley Twins #23, **CLAIM TO FAME.**

YOUR OWN

SLAM BOOK!

If you've read *Slambook Fever*, Sweet Valley High #48, you know that slam books are the rage at Sweet Valley High. Now *you* can have a slam book of your own! Make up your own categories, such as "Biggest Jock" or "Best Looking," and have your friends fill in the rest! There's a four-page calendar, horoscopes and questions most asked by Sweet Valley readers with answers from Elizabeth and Jessica

Watch for FRANCINE PASCAL'S SWEET VALLEY HIGH SLAM BOOK, on sale in September. It's a must for SWEET VALLEY fans!

☐ 05496-1 FRANCINE PASCAL'S SWEET VALLEY HIGH
        SLAM BOOK
        Laurie Pascal Wenk $3.50

- -

IT ALL STARTED WITH

THE

SWEET VALLEY TWINS

For two years teenagers across the U.S. have been reading about Jessica and Elizabeth Wakefield and their High School friends in SWEET VALLEY HIGH books. Now in books created especially for you, author Francine Pascal introduces you to Jessica and Elizabeth when they were 12, facing the same problems with their folks and friends that you do.